S0-AJW-078

COWBOY IN THE MAKING

Books by Will James

*

THE AMERICAN COWBOY

HORSES I'VE KNOWN

THE DARK HORSE

FLINT SPEARS

SCORPION

HOME RANCH

THE THREE MUSTANGEERS

ALL IN THE DAY'S RIDING

BIG-ENOUGH

SUN UP

LONE COWBOY

SAND

COW COUNTRY

SMOKY, THE COWHORSE

THE DRIFTING COWBOY

COWBOYS, NORTH AND SOUTH

The Uncle Bill Series

UNCLE BILL: A TALE OF TWO KIDS
AND A COWBOY

IN THE SADDLE WITH UNCLE BILL

LOOK-SEE WITH UNCLE BILL

*

YOUNG COWBOY

COWBOY IN THE MAKING

MY FIRST HORSE

*

CHARLES SCRIBNER'S SONS

A Cowboy in the Making

COWBOY IN THE MAKING

BY

WILL JAMES

ARRANGED FROM THE FIRST
CHAPTERS OF "LONE COWBOY"

ILLUSTRATED BY THE AUTHOR

CHARLES SCRIBNER'S SONS · NEW YORK
CHARLES SCRIBNER'S SONS · LTD · LONDON

1945

Copyright, 1937, by
CHARLES SCRIBNER'S SONS

Printed in the United States of America

*All rights reserved. No part of this book
may be reproduced in any form without
the permission of Charles Scribner's Sons*

CONTENTS

All Points West –
June 6, 1937

Dear Reader –

This is of the early story of my life, when I was a kid and about half as tall as my long rifle – The most of it I'd like to live over again, especially when old Bopy and me would drift south after a long winter's trapping in the far north and I would see my little horse again – shed off my moccasins, slip on my copper-toed boots and go to riding alongside or ahead of the wagon Bopy would be driving, going still further south and headed for the heart of the cow country –

The experiences I had with Bopy, and what all the wise old trapper taught me stood one in good stead many a time and place afterwards – It was a sure enough outdoor schooling but it also got to fitting well between walls or anywhere –

Stay with your lessons, kids, but get outside and learn all you can about animals, specially the horse, he's your best friend –

Sincerely –
WILL JAMES
'37

I

A COWBOY COMES TO MONTANA

ONE JUNE DAY some years ago a wagon pulled by four tired horses came to a stop among the trees bordering a little creek in Montana. The young woman who had been driving the team climbed down off the wagon seat and threw the lines to one side. The horses would stand, they'd be glad to.

On the same trail, a quarter of a mile back, rode

a long lean cowboy with ten saddle horses. As he saw the wagon stop he left them to graze and loped up to where the woman was busy unhooking the team.

"Now, Bonnie," he said, as he slid off his horse, "don't you go to bothering with that." He smiled at her. "I'll show you what *you* can do."

He climbed into the wagon, yanked out a roll of bedding and slid it to the ground. Pointing to the bedding he said:

"This is what you can do, Bonnie. Stretch out on that and rest up while I unhook the team."

"But I ought to start setting up camp, Bill."

Bill frowned and smiled. "You do as I tell you, Bonnie." He unhooked the team, fed the horses and turned them loose. A comfortable camp was made while Bonnie looked on.

"We ought to make the town tomorrow or early next day, Bonnie," said Bill.

But it was many days before the town was reached, for that night I came into the world. I was born close to the sod, and if I could have seen much my

THE ARRIVAL IN MONTANA

first day I'd have glimpsed ponies through the flap of the tent. And if I heard anything it was the bellering of cattle and the ringing of my dad's spurs.

My dad was a cowboy from Texas. He figured that it was good cow country up north and he and my mother were heading for Alberta, Canada, to start in the cow business up there. Then I came along and stopped the outfit in Montana. If I'd been born a month later I'd be a Canadian, and four months sooner would have made me a Texan.

But anyway, whatever I would have been, I was sure good in holding up the outfit. It didn't move for many days, but as soon as possible my dad hooked up the team again and slow and easy took us to town. After a spell there we drifted on north some more and my dad found a cow outfit to work for where my mother and I had a good roof over our heads. He'd given up the idea of going any further north for the time being, and when fall began to set in he decided to winter where he was. In Montana.

It was along the next spring when my mother took down with some sort of cold which today I guess is called the grippe, and soon after that my dad found himself with no one but just me.

My dad got wild and reckless when my mother went, and her death came near being his own too. I was all that kept him from doing things that sure would have killed him. Fast action and danger made him forget the hurt he packed in his heart.

And fast action and danger was what he went after. With the big rough horses he'd go and pile his rope on everything that was wild and needed roping, and lots of big stuff that didn't need roping. Many a cowboy held his breath at watching the "fool things" he'd do.

II

FIRST RIDING

I DIDN'T see much of my dad that summer, only for a day or so about once or twice a month. He had left me in care of a couple who were running a small outfit on the outskirt of the range he rode on. They had no children and were mighty glad to have me.

It was there that the Old Timer used to come to see me and rest his horses while visiting. He seemed to know my dad mighty well, and what I know of my early childhood is what the Old Timer gave me. I remember him as early as I do my dad. He was on the job when I started to walk and when I started to talk. I called him "Bopy." That was as close as I could get to saying "Beaupré" which was what the folks on the ranch called him.

Jean Beaupré was his name, or one of his names, as I found out years later. My dad called him Trapper Jean. That's what he was, a trapper during winters, and he'd try prospecting for gold during the summers. He was a French Canadian from away up in the far Northwest Country. He could talk many Indian languages and sign talk all mixed with French. French was his main language and he could talk very little English.

Sometimes the Old Timer would bring me a chipmunk in a cage he'd made, or a squirrel. He always kept me supplied with horned toads, young woodchucks, young beavers, and even young porcupines. The young porcupines didn't stay long, as soon as the quills began to show they somehow or other disappeared. Most of the young animals I had made good pets and a few of them stayed around the ranch even after they were full grown.

My dad took on a contract breaking horses. He stayed at a ranch, but as there was no one there to take care of me he left me where I was. Once a week or so he'd ride over on some big snorting bronk and stay overnight.

But the horse breaking contract didn't pan out so good. He'd been pretty well bruised up being so wild the summer before. And then one day, about Christmas time, a stump-headed bronk bucks off the side of a mountain with him, turns over and leaves him in a willow thicket at the bottom. One of the boys finds him there just by pure luck, brings him in and takes him to the hospital. He lay there between sheets until away into the next summer and when he came out he couldn't afford to be wild at all for the rest of that summer. He was with me most of the time then and I got to know him again.

That summer was my first time on a horse, for as soon as my dad could ride a gentle horse he'd hoist me up on top with him. I'd sit on the saddle behind him and hang on to his cartridge belt. We used to go on powerful long rides that way.

I didn't feel so good when my dad left me again that fall. I pegged along sort of lonesome. He couldn't come and see me very often and, to make things worse, the Old Timer had left for the far north into Canada where he set his traps. I liked the folks I was with a whole lot, but I liked my dad first and the Old Timer second. I wasn't getting so much riding when my dad was gone, and I wasn't getting so many pets as when the Old Timer was around. But the folks tried to make up for that as best they could. A wooden horse on rockers was made for me. That's one of the first things I remember. The body was hewed out of a cotton wood log and painted gray and there was a real horse mane and tail on him. I had a lot of fun saddling and unsaddling him with an old sawbuck pack saddle tree. Then Mommy, as I called the lady there, was a great hand at calling me in often and handing me things to eat which I had a weakness for.

A stump-headed bronk bucks off the side of a mountain with him

First Riding

I had some more fun down by the corrals and stables, too. I had a piece of light rope and I'd try to rope chickens. Then I'd go to the pig pen, and calf pen, and play horse by the mangers in the stable. I'd put a halter around my neck, stick some hay in my mouth, then nicker and stamp my feet. I'd snort, too, and pull back like a bronk.

But with all of that play I was lonesome. I was often calling for someone, and I'd sit down for long spells and just star gaze. It was during those lonesome spells that I would pick up things and want to make marks, tracing something in the dirt with a stick. Or with a hunk of charcoal, I'd pick up from the last fire at the branding pen, I'd go and mark up the rough boards of the bunk house porch. That winter, when the cold winds blew outside and the snow piled up so I couldn't go out, was when I first got acquainted with a pencil and some blank paper. I spent many hours a day making funny marks which, to anybody else, didn't mean anything, but to me meant a lot. To me they were all pictures of animals, mostly horses. My dad would say they were sure fine and once in a while he'd criticize and pass such re-marks as, "The hind legs on that horse are a little too straight, son" or, "You forgot dewclaws on that steer."

When spring came, my dad rode up again and I can remember how glad I was when I saw the white tarpaulin of his bed hitched on to the horse he was leading. That meant he'd be with me more than a day or so, and, sure enough, he was with me about a month.

I think the greatest surprise and pleasure of my life was when he took his roll of bedding off the pack horse, after he rode in the evening, for under the bed was a little bitty saddle that looked just like a full size one, and just my fit. My dad lifted me up on it and he said,

"This is your outfit, son, this horse and this saddle."

I was so tickled I just hollered and threw both my feet up on the pony's withers.

The horse, as I remember, was a little long-maned black. I don't think he weighed over six hundred.

THE HORSE, AS I REMEMBERED, WAS A LITTLE LONG-MANED BLACK

First Riding

He was as round as a butter ball and gentle as a kitten, but the saddle was what interested me the most.

I'd already seen lots of horses, but a saddle like the one I had, all for my own self, struck me as a gift that even Santa Claus couldn't compete with in handing out. There was even a brand new rope on it. I know that night was long for me and I was sure watching for daybreak so I could get out and try my horse and rigging. They had a hard time getting me to eat that morning.

Dad and I took many a good ride together that month. I was with him steady, except when he'd be gone for an all day ride. Then I'd hit out by myself. The little black horse had to be shod and fed lots of grain so he could stand up under the work I was giving him. There came a time when they had to give me a fresh horse while the black rested.

I sure was a happy kid, and to make things even better, the Old Timer drifted in one day. He'd long ago sold his furs from the winter's trapping and come South again. But I wasn't looking for more pets just then. I was very busy with my horse and my saddle and my rope. With my dad's and the Old Timer's company to fill in, I had my hands full. There was one month when I hardly touched a pencil or tried to make marks on anything. I sure wasn't lonesome any more.

My dad had given up the idea of going to Canada to start for himself again, for, as he told the Old Timer, he couldn't think of settling anywhere or building any home, with my mother gone. He meant to keep on riding for the outfits around here and there, keep saving his wages, and some day, when I got big enough, to start me out with a good cow outfit of my own.

But that never came true, and when he left me after that great month we had together I never saw him again.

There was quite a herd of cattle in the corral where he was working and amongst that herd was a big steer that had just broken a horn in the shute. The blood from that broken horn was running down that steer's face to his nose, and he was on the fight, not with his own breed but with anything strange, like a human. [16]

Some day I would have a cow outfit of my own

He saw my dad standing there and my dad, being busy prodding cattle thru the shute, wasn't paying any attention. He'd just stooped down for the prodding stick he'd dropped when the big steer caught him broadside with his one good horn, hoisted him in the air, took him on a ways and then flung him against the chutes.

The cowboys rushed to him, but, so they told the Old Timer, they saw at a glance that nothing could be done. But, they said, there was a smile on my dad's face when after a while he opened his eyes and the first words he said were: "Well, boys, I'm due to join her soon now." Then, after a while, he added on, "The only thing I regret is to leave little Billy behind. . . . Tell old trapper Jean that all my gatherings are his and to see that my boy is well took care of. I leave him to him."

He talked on for a little while and within an hour from the time the steer had picked him up he closed his eyes and went on the Long Sleep.

III

THE OLD TIMER TAKES ME ALONG

NO ONE told me of my dad's going, not for many months. All I was told was that he'd taken a herd across the border and that no one knew when he'd be back.

I kept asking every once in a while when my dad would be back, and I'd always get the same answer, "I don't know, Billy, but he ought to be back most any week now." I kept on asking until, finally, nearly a year later, the Old Timer had to let me know.

The Old Timer Takes Me Along

I can't begin to tell you just how I took the news. I couldn't play at anything. Many a time I'd hit out back of the corrals where nobody could see me, lie flat on the ground and have a cry.

Then one evening in late spring, the Old Timer told me that we'd be hitting out with a pack outfit early in the morning. We'd drift on and on and see all kinds of country and lots of things I'd never seen before. That interested me some, but not in any way like it should have.

But the Old Timer was wise. He knew that the new country with all the new sights would be good medicine for me. The next morning I kissed Mommy goodbye, shook hands with Lem, her husband, got on my horse and started out alongside of the Old Timer.

We camped out that night and the interest I took in being in the way when I was really trying to help, was a good start towards making me forget. We picketed the ponies, that is I picketed my own anyway, even if the Old Timer did have to look over the knots I'd tied.

Supper of fried beef and fried potatoes, biscuits and coffee sure tasted good even if there was no butter. After supper was over, we both reared back against the bed roll and watched the fire. I felt pretty big for a five year old.

Pretty soon the Old Timer began to talk. He said something about us going to the other side of the mountain. He pointed it out to me. It looked very far away and the setting sun was coloring the peaks of it. The Old Timer went on talking, and then I knew that we were going to be partners, partners for good, and that made me feel bigger. He told me what my dad had said before he died, and I knew then why he took me away. This wasn't going to be any little camping trip and I was glad, for I liked to roam. Next to my dad there was no one I would rather have roamed with than the Old Timer.

I don't know how I slept that first night out. I think I was awake at daybreak looking towards that tall mountain to the west. I must have wondered what it looked like on the other side, because that was natural with me. I've been wondering what it

STARTED OUT ALONGSIDE OF THE OLD TIMER

looks like on the other side of every mountain and hill ever since.

I was glad to get breakfast over and see the outfit packed so we could start out. It took us a couple of days to get up in a pass of the tall mountain. There was a lot of snow up there, and from that pass we could see at least a hundred miles both ways to some more mountains. Bopy stopped there a while. I looked all around and got to feeling littler and littler. Finally I said,

"Gosh a'mighty, Bopy, if the world is as big on the other side of them mountains as what I can see of it on this side, it sure is a powerful big world!"

We rode down the mountain through twisted trees, and finally through a forest of big tall straight trees. I sure liked them. We saw two deer and a big porcupine and I looked for Bopy to reach for his rifle, but he didn't and we watched the deer as long as we could. I'd seen quite a few dead deer brought in the ranch but these were the first live ones I'd seen and they struck me as being mighty well worth watching.

That night we camped in a grassy meadow where

a little stream ran through. We went further on down country the next day and by noon we came to a deserted dug-out cabin. A corral was close to it, a good creek, lots of grass and timber. We made camp there, not in the cabin because a pack rat had taken that and built a big nest in the center of it and it would have been a lot of work cleaning out. Besides we liked it better outside.

We camped by the dug-out for a few days. Bopy wasted a lot of time by the fire, cooking different things, things he thought I'd like and which I was used to getting at the ranch.

When I wasn't watching Bopy cooking, or getting in the way with my trying to help, I'd go over to the dug-out and watch for the pack rat. But I never could see him, so one time I took a stick and began scattering the big pile of bark and chips and small sticks that his home was made of. Bopy caught me at that and stopped me, asking how I would like to be left out in the cold snow without a home when winter came.

That night the pack rat visited our camp, chewed

two latigoes off one of the pack saddles to pieces and put them on top of his pile. The pack rat is also called a trade rat, and for every piece of the latigo he brought back a chip or a small stick. There was quite a bunch of these around the pack saddle.

Every day Bopy was gone as long as two or three hours. He was prospecting for gold, and he went out with a prospector's pick in one hand and a rifle in the other. Sometimes I went with him. A new sport or country always interested me and I'd prowl around looking for holes to dig into. I picked up pretty rocks like Bopy did and stacked them up so we could take 'em to camp like he did the ones he'd find. I couldn't understand why he would never take mine.

I'd watch the squirrels, birds and rabbits. They'd let me get pretty close and there were lots of them around. When I got tired of fooling, I'd go by my horse and sometimes go to sleep.

My horse was a lot of company to me. I used to like to fool around his legs and chest as high as I could reach, and feel the muscles under the smooth hide. I guess that's where I got my first lessons, and plenty more afterwards, in the anatomy of a horse and the reason why I draw horses without even once sketching one from life.

In the forenoons after a day's prospecting and collecting ore samples, Bopy would go to work assaying. He'd take his pan to the creek, pound his rocks to a powder. Then he'd put the powder in the pan, add some water and work the pan in a slow circling motion, letting out a little of the crushed rock with every one of the motions. If there was any particle of gold or heavy mineral in the ore it would stay in the bottom of the pan.

He would take a lot of time doing that, and once in a while I'd hear him say he'd "struck it." Later on when he'd get a chance to send a sample of the ore to a town assayer he'd always get reports that it would be too far to haul, and that would make him leave the land unclaimed.

Sometimes when he was working I'd begin to think of my dad again and feel sort of alone. Then I'd rummage through the panniers of the pack outfit hoping I'd find something I could draw on. Drawing relieved me of things that were in me which words couldn't put out. I was always at peace when I was drawing.

But I couldn't find a scrap of paper of any kind, not even as big as my thumb nail. Bopy caught me searching one day and asked me what I was looking for and I told him. . . .

IV

PAPER AND PENCIL

WE MOVED camp the next day early, and we didn't poke along as we usually did. It was just after noon when we came to a fence and further down, about half a mile, I could see houses and corrals. Bopy stopped, tied up the two pack horses and told me to stay right there with 'em, that he'd be gone just a little while. Then he rode away towards the gate that opened the fence into the ranch.

When he came back he had a smile on his face that was a yard wide. He didn't explain to me what he'd gone to the ranch for. Instead, he reached for a little canvas bag that was tied on one of the packs and pulled out half a dozen long strips of "jerky" (dried meat). He handed me a couple and we went to chewing. That was our dinner for that day and we ate as we rode.

We camped that night and I'll always remember that one morning when I woke up and, moseying around as usual, went to where my saddle was. On top of the saddle was a big thick tablet of writing paper. It was the first I'd seen that wasn't lined, or was so white. Alongside of it were two pencils. They were also the longest I'd ever seen.

It was hard to get me to breakfast that morning and I didn't take the time to eat much of it when I got there. I was still chewing on my last bite when I went to my pencils and tablet again. I was so anxious that I couldn't draw half as well as I did when I was at the ranch. I was just like a fellow wanting to talk too fast and trying to put ten words in the time of one.

But I wasn't wasting any paper, and if I did make

wild drawings I sure used up all the space on one side of the sheet and the same on the other. I was just beginning to cool down when Bopy comes along, peeks over my shoulder and tells me he's going to be very busy today and I'd better stay in camp and watch things. He pointed to the fire and showed me the hole where the little dutch oven was that held the noon meal. It was a stew he'd started the night before and the little oven had low coals round it to keep it warm. All I'd have to do would be to scrape the ashes off the lid, lift it off and help myself. There were cold biscuits and a creekful of cold water to go along with that.

After all the instructions were handed out, Bopy picked up his prospector's pick, his rifle and some jerky and away he went.

I lay flat on the ground and, propped on my elbows, hat away back on my head, I drew until the sun, beating on my backbone, made me hunt a tree for shade. With my back against the tree and using my knees for a table I drew some more.

The sun went past high center and I was still

drawing. The time was near middle afternoon when an empty feeling in the pit of my stomach reminded me that there were other things besides drawing that

I LAY FLAT ON THE GROUND

needed attention. When I finally put my tablet and pencil down and looked toward the spot where the oven was buried, my appetite hit me full force. My breakfast had been kind of light.

[31]

I managed to get some ashes into the stew as I lifted the lid, but I made a good meal just the same and I went to drawing some more that afternoon. When Bopy came back to camp I was glad to see him, for my hankering for drawing had been satisfied considerable and now I was ready for talk.

I went right into drawing the next morning, but only for a couple of hours. I began to find lots of faults with the drawings I'd done the day before, and which I'd thought so fine then. The ones I did the second day struck me as worse. So, for the time being, I put my tablet and pencils carefully away and went to the creek to watch Bopy pan his dirt.

My drawing from then on was kind of in spells. I went along with Bopy on prospecting trips and seldom would my tablet and pencils hold me in camp. By this time I was having my hands full taking in everything that interested me and I was beginning to forget my lonesomeness for the love of a mother and the steady companionship of a father.

V

WINTER CAMP

BOPY and I covered many a mile that summer and we set up many a camp in many a different place. The Old Timer had quite a pile of "sample rock" by then. None of it was much good, and when the reports came back from the assayer's office, old Bopy began to look for a camp again where the fur trapping was good.

The camp was one of Bopy's own, one of the many he'd built himself. It was late in the fall when we came to it. The grass had turned to a yellow brown and the frost was beginning to color up the trees. We turned the ponies loose in a fenced pasture. We didn't leave the skillets or bedding outside because we'd struck a home camp where we were to hole-up for the winter.

Inside of the camp, a dirt-roofed, one-roomed log cabin, was a long wide bunk. Under it were about a hundred traps of all sizes. But the traps didn't interest me as much as what I'd spotted in one corner of the cabin. There, all stacked up, was a pile of magazines and books.

I don't know how old the magazines were, and I didn't care, because I couldn't read anyway. The pictures were what took my eye. They were pictures of all things I'd never seen and which were as strange to me as anything strange could be. I remember seeing pictures of people dressed in clothes of the kind I'd never seen before, whiskers cut sort of queer, pretty women, with lots of hair, and ponies without tails or manes.

Bopy spent many a long evening explaining all

BOPY SPENT MANY A LONG EVENING EXPLAINING

that stumped me in the pictures. After he got through I still didn't understand, for I'd never seen what the pictures pictured. I'd never seen much beyond the ranch and the plains and the mountains and the places where we camped.

The trees went bare of leaves, snows came and covered up the grass, a dry log shelter was built for the ponies and hay was stacked up outside. Bopy dug out his traps, and scattered them on the trail. It was then something happened which held up my growth considerable.

Some animal was robbing Bopy's traps, killing and eating most all that'd been caught in 'em, and Bopy set out to catch that animal. He washed three or four traps so they wouldn't give any scent, using a mixture of lye and something else. When he got through there was no scent to any trap.

But Bopy had overlooked something. That was me. He'd left that strong mixture in a lid of a can on the floor and I happened to see it. He was gone for just one minute—I think, maybe just to hang a trap, but in that time I took hold of that lid. What was inside of it looked to me like sirup, so I drank it down.

It all went down smooth enough but a short spell afterwards, maybe a few seconds, an awful pain hit my middle. Bopy came in, looked at me and looked at the lid. Then he was on the job. With his skinning knife he tore the top off a can of condensed milk and poured the whole contents down my throat. I well remember the biting of that lye, but I also remember the soothing of that milk. It stayed down me about one minute and then it came up and out. A doctor said afterwards that was all that could have saved me.

That winter was a painful one. I lay and groaned and I wasn't caring for my tablet of white paper, my pony saddle or rope or any of the magazines that were stacked up in the corner.

Bopy didn't get many furs that winter. He never left me alone for more than two hours at a time and always he'd run back like the house was afire. I must have been a lot of worry to him because I was a pretty sick kid and hard to get along with. Maybe sometimes Bopy wished he'd left me at the ranch, but I don't hardly think so. His actions never showed that, he did whatever he could for me and always with a smile showing through his whiskers.

"Comment es-tu, Billee?" (How are you, Billy?) he would always ask as he'd come in from his trap line. He'd bring in the fresh-skinned hides to stretch, close the door as quick as he could, stir up the fire and see that I was warm, and then he'd go to talking, telling me some of his experiences of that day.

By that time he'd got so he talked to me always in French. Only once in a while he would bring in a few words of English, just when I couldn't understand the French.

It was along towards spring when the pains began to ease up inside of me and I began to take an interest in anything again. Gradually I'd get a little deeper into the stack of magazines in the corner, and stay longer. Then I started using my pen and pencils some more.

It was about then, when I began to perk up some, that Bopy took it upon himself to teach me to read.

He had lots of time on his hands because the trapping season was well past. One day we'd work on letters and the next day on numbers, and Bopy saw to it, once he got me started, that I did at least an hour's studying every day.

That was the start of my schooling from the only teacher I ever had. I took to grammar natural-like and I got so it was very seldom I misspelt a word.

It was late that summer before I could set on my horse and be comfortable again. By that time I'd got along pretty well with my education and I could make out and write quite a few fair-sized words, but that was all left aside when I got to riding again. I'd been too sick to miss my horse and outfit that winter and spring, and it wasn't till I got in my little saddle on the little black's back and uncoiling my rope once more that I lost all interest in books and reading and writing, even drawing.

It sure tickled old Bopy to see me on my horse again, and he used to grin and tell me I looked a heap better in the saddle now I wasn't so fat.

WILL JAMES

VI

COWBOYS AGAIN

I REMEMBER especially the first winter Bopy and I passed with a cow outfit. Fall was creeping on, snow was on the peaks of the mountains and Bopy began to look for a place where there'd be a solid roof over our heads for the winter, and solid walls around us.

One day we came to what looked to me like a town, only there were no tall buildings. They were all low, dirt-roofed log houses, long and rambling. There were many corrals, round ones, square ones, and all shapes. There were long strings of stables, sheds, shelters, and many hundred head of cattle and horses in some of the corrals.

It was just getting dark when Bopy pulled up in front of one of the long log houses. A cowboy came out and said, "Get down, strangers, and put your ponies away. You can leave your bed right here." Bopy didn't say a word and did as the cowboy told him to. We fed our ponies hay that night.

I don't know how big my eyes were but I know they were sure full size when we got back and went in the door of the long log house. It was the first real bunk house I'd seen. All around the house was a double deck of bunks built to the wall. There must have been at least thirty of them. At each end of the house was a long box stove that could take a three foot log. Between the stoves were three tables and over each one was a big hanging kerosene lamp.

But the lay of the bunk house wasn't what interested me most as I first walked in there with Bopy. It was the boys. About ten cowboys were warming up by the stove. They'd just come in from a cold day's ride and were talking of that day's work and

AT EACH END OF THE HOUSE WAS A LONG BOX STOVE

what had to be done tomorrow. They edged to one side as we came in, to give us room by the stove.

Now more cowboys kept coming in every few minutes. When the bell rang and all trailed out towards the chuck house, I know I counted about twenty riders. We had bumped into the main camp of a big cow outfit. And big it was sure enough. I remember Bopy telling me later there was on an average of eighty cowboys working the year round on that "spread" (cow outfit). Each rider had from eight to twelve horses, and the outfit ranged upwards of a hundred thousand head of cattle.

I wish I could remember some of the talk and stories that went around that evening, when all gathered in the bunk house again after the meal.

The next morning I went to moseying around the corrals and stables and when I came to one of the corrals where a lot of the boys were working, I camped right there, got inside the corral and forgot time. They were separating horses and running the ones they wanted, or didn't want, into another corral. Some of them had to be roped and dragged out.

In another corral they were separating cattle by the help of a chute. I stopped there for a while and then went on to another corral where two riders were busy taming unbroken horses. There I stayed and stayed. I stayed till four or five bronks were topped off in their first saddling. When the boys began to talk to me and grinned, I could never begin to think of leaving. And I didn't know but what we'd just had breakfast when the dinner bell rang.

Bopy was at the table when I went in and he grinned at me when I came in with the two bronk busters. He sure hadn't been idle. He'd been up to see one of the main heads of the outfit, inquired as to how trapping was in the neighborhood and the answer had been that it was good, too good. Too many varmints, like big coyotes, part gray wolf, were killing many young calves every spring. The result was that Bopy was offered all the grub and traps and everything he needed, and wages to boot, if he would only take one of the cow camps on the company's range and do his best to catch all the varmints he could.

Taming a tough one

Cowboys Again

The next morning early we pulled out with quite an outfit of our own. One of the ranch hands came along to drive the team and bring it back, and Bopy and I rode behind the wagon, bringing up the pack horses.

I hated to leave the ranch, but after a while I was made to understand that we would ride back again some time and stay a few days. That eased my feeling some and I began to look forward as to what kind of a camp it was we were going to. When we got there late that night I didn't care to investigate and see what kind of a place it was, not right then. I went to sleep till Bopy called me to eat. It seemed that right after I got thru eating it was morning again.

WILL JAMES

VII

THE COW CAMP

THE COW CAMP, as I looked it over the next morning, turned out to be quite a place. There was a well-chinked two-roomed log house that Bopy was busy throwing bucket after bucket of water into and sweeping out afterwards. The camp hadn't been used for a couple of winters.

I moseyed on down to the corrals. There were lots of them, enough corrals to hold a couple of thousand head of stock. There were chutes too, and bronk pens with snubbing posts and a slaughter pen with a hoisting wheel. I had a lot of fun in the corrals. I'd play wild horse by the hour, put a rope around my shoulders—I knew better than putting it around my neck—and after fastening myself to the snubbing post and giving myself plenty of slack, I'd run as fast as I could until the rope jerked me to a stop. Then, like I'd seen the bronks do at the ranch, I'd turn and snort and paw the air or throw myself.

I think I had a natural interest in watching animals, what they did and how they might have felt. I liked to see a big herd and watch the cowboys work, brand and round 'em up, but to me cattle were just beef, an animal to raise and ship to market and set up on the table in a big platter, smoking hot. With a horse it's very different, he's a partner to work with, and I think I felt that from the first.

I sure got back to being cowboy again that winter. The visit at the ranch had stirred up what was in my blood. My rope began to get a lot of use. While riding my little black, I'd run by a post or a brush and throw my loop at it. Sometimes I'd catch what I threw at and sometimes what I'd catch would be pretty solid. Then, my rope being tied hard and fast to my saddle horn, I'd get quite a jerk when my pony hit the end. I'd come near to falling off many a time.

It was thru that winter that I began getting a little flesh back on my bones. Outside of feeling a little sick at the stomach once in a while at meal time, I'd pretty well got over the effects of drinking the lye.

What helped to make the winter good was that once in a while a cowboy or two would drop in, put his horse in the stable and stay overnight. With the visits of the cowboys, the fun I had playing, and once in a while going with Bopy on his trap lines, then my drawing, reading and writing and all, I don't remember one lonesome minute. Bopy had been thoughtful enough to include a big stack of magazines with the load of grub and grain.

Bopy had a good winter, too. He had over a hundred big coyote pelts to show for his work, not counting a few badger and bobcat pelts.

I LIKED TO WATCH THE COWBOYS WORK

My drawing wasn't neglected—I never did neglect that for very long. During the long winter evenings, or when it was storming too hard to be out, I spent many an hour making things on my tablet with my pencil. Most of my drawings were of horses, about four out of every five. I'd draw them running, standing and bucking, and from all angles, most of the time with a cowboy setting on top of them with a rope in his hand, and maybe a few cattle somewhere around. From the start I always liked to draw something with a little story in it. It always made it more interesting for me to draw while trying to put that story over.

When I'd draw a horse I'd a lot of times stick in a bear or a wolf for him to spook up at or run away from. Or I'd have horses or cattle drifting with the storm and maybe a rider alongside, like I'd once in a while seen that winter.

I kept most of the drawings I thought good at the time I made 'em. They'd be shabby at the edges and crinkled from being packed. Sometimes I'd sure surprise myself at the improvement I'd made. I'd laugh at the old ones and show them to Bopy, who agreed with me that the new ones were better. Then I'd tear up most of the old ones.

My education, my drawing, my roping and riding had improved considerable by the time the range was bare of snow and grass was long enough to keep our horses in shape when traveling. Then, as usual, away we went. As Bopy promised me, we went to the ranch first and stayed there a few days.

Those few days at the ranch were more than enjoyed by me. I'd be handed a horse every day, always a new one, and it was hard for the cowboys to leave me behind on any short ride. I think I had just as much fun with them as they did with me, and that's saying a lot. If, when bringing in some cattle or horses, an animal broke out, I was always hollered at to "head 'er off, cowboy." Most of the time I could do that, when they weren't too wild. I'd work with the boys at the chutes and in the corrals and I don't know how much in the way I was. None of the boys ever said, and I'd often hear one tell Bopy how I was sure making quite a hand of myself.

Whether that was true or not, I'd feel mighty pleased and proud.

There's no use saying that I hated to leave that ranch. I hated to more than I can tell, and maybe I showed it so that the foreman thought something ought to be done about it. He grabbed me by the back of the neck, took me to the corrals with him, waved his hand towards the many saddle horses in one of the corrals, and told me to take my pick. I pointed out a little gray horse, he reminded me some of a toy horse I'd had. The foreman looked where I was pointing. Then laughed and shook his head, saying that I was pretty poor at picking out a good horse. Then he took down his rope, made a loop, and dabbed it onto a fat little sorrel with a white mane and tail. I hadn't seen him among all the other horses and he was sure a surprise and picture to look at as he was led out to me. He was even prettier than my little black and, as I found out afterwards, just as quick and fast. I was sure well mounted from that day on.

My interest in running my fingers thru the white

mane of that little sorrel horse did a lot to keep me from looking back as we left the ranch. After we got out a few days I settled right down to looking ahead again and wondering what was on the other side of every ridge and mountain.

WILL JAMES

VIII

DRIFTING NORTH

BOPY and I kept drifting north. One day in our
drifting Bopy stops the outfit by an iron post
standing all by itself on a ridge. He steps off the
wagon, and I steps off my horse and we gather by
that post. It was the dividing mark between the
U. S. A. and Canada.

Bopy points to the south from that post and waves an arm and says, "C'est ton pays, mon enfant" (that's your country, my child"). Then he waved to the north and said that was his. But, as I understood him to say then, he wasn't so free in that country and I'd have to be careful not to mention the name of Jean Beaupré from now on. There was no danger of me mentioning the name of Jean Beaupré because I could hardly ever remember that name and I never called him by any other than Bopy.

As I found out later, from Bopy himself, the reason he was so careful was that he was wanted up there for some things he'd done years before, some mixups he'd got into. He didn't come out and tell me of any killings, but whatever it was he was wanted for, sure must have been serious because the authorities wouldn't have been still looking for him if the mixups had been plain fights. But knowing Bopy as I did, I know that whatever he'd done that might have been against the law, sure was something he couldn't help doing, or where he figured he was in the right.

I used to wonder why Bopy would take the chance of going into a country where he was wanted and liable to get caught when he could just as well have stayed south of the line where he was a lot safer. One day he told me. It was that the trapping was so much better to the north and besides the part of the country where he was taking any chance of being caught was only a few hundred miles wide. Once he got into the north woods he felt safe again.

"And there's not much danger now," he'd say. "Them troubles he come long tam ago."

I liked that country. To me there's no place like the open prairie to see a sunset or a sunrise from. We moseyed along pretty slow through the prairie country and whenever we'd come to some good creek or river we'd camp for days at a time.

It was middle summer when we got into rolling timber land. One day we ran into a used road cutting across the forest and we began to pass teams and wagons going and coming. We made camp by a little lake that night and next morning Bopy shaved again. Then he put on a clean shirt and clean pants and he told me to change my outfit, too. It was noon that day when, in a big clearing, we ran into a town of log and frame houses. The sight of that town was sure some surprise to me when Bopy headed for the center of it. I sat my horse tight and wished for about a dozen eyes so I could take in the sights. It was the first town I'd seen.

As I remember the town now it must have been small and there might have been about fifty people in sight all along the wide street, but it looked to me like thousands. We passed a few store windows and that sure got my eye, but what got my eye most was when I spotted two little boys about my size, playing at the back end of a wagon.

I'd never figured out there were little people like me, all I'd ever seen was big people like my dad, Bopy and the cowboys. The boys jabbered at me as I rode by, and stared too, but they weren't staring at me, they were staring at my horse and outfit. They'd never seen such an outfit before. That wasn't a cow country, too cold and too much snow and timber. No cowboys came so far north and nobody hardly ever rode.

That's how the kids were so curious about my and Bopy's outfit, but I don't think they were near as curious about our outfits as I was about them. They came along and followed us. Pretty soon half a dozen other kids joined them and one little one was dressed just like I remember Mommy dressing. Of the dozen kids that gathered that one with the skirts held most of my attention. It was the first girl I'd ever seen.

Bopy and I went around to town to a trader's post. It was the first store I'd ever been into, and while Bopy went to buying supplies, I was sure busy looking around at all the strange things. When I was looking around somebody handed me a striped stick and I didn't know what to do with it. I looked at the stick, and then at the person who handed it to me. When that person saw I didn't know what it was, I was told to lick it. I did, and with that sweet tasting stick and my interest for all that was around I don't think I could have had more use for my senses. I saw some more little people too, and I let one suck on my stick of candy for a spell.

We stayed that night in a real hotel, it was a two floor building and made of logs. It struck me as mighty stuffy in there after being so used to sleeping outside, and I didn't sleep well. Besides I wanted to be out and looking around. I wanted to see some more of the little people.

We were out early the next morning and after breakfast we hit out for the stable. There I received a shock. All our pack outfit, grub and all, was in a wagon, all but the pack saddles. I looked out to see our horses in a pasture, then Bopy told me the news.

He told me that from now on I wasn't a cowboy, not for a spell anyway, and that I was to ride in a wagon driven by a freighter and that all our horses would be left behind for the winter. Bopy tried to grin and say that in a joking way, but it didn't go well with me. I sure hated to leave my outfit. Poor Bopy did his best to explain why that had to be. He said that the snow would be too deep for horses where he was going and that no horse could live there thru the winter. The stable man would take good care of 'em and we would have them again as soon as spring came.

I couldn't even take my rope along, for, as Bopy said, "Every ounce of weight will sure count when

we get to where the team and wagon can go no further." We'd still have to go a couple of hundred
miles after that. I also had to take off the boots which
Bopy had got me that spring and put on a heavy pair
of laced shoes. I sure felt disgraced for good then,
for here I was just like anybody else.

As we started out of town I hid down in the
bottom of the wagon so none of the kids would see
me in such a disgraceful way and I didn't show up
until we were well out.

We traveled many days after that, following a
rough road that had been bedded over with a thick
layer of branches.

The country was pretty, the trees had been touched
by the first frosts and they were all colors, but I
didn't like it anything like the range land we'd left
to the south. This was no cow country, there were
no ranches and no riders and a man had to turn pack
horse.

We got to the end of the wagon road, unloaded
the wagon and the next morning the freighter pulled
out.

Bopy made two packs, one for him and one for

me. Mine sure looked small as compared to his, and I tried to add on more. Bopy wouldn't let me, he said it'd be plenty heavy enough by sundown.

I don't know how much I packed on that first trip, I don't think any more than fifteen pounds, and I found that Bopy had been right when he said it'd get plenty heavy enough by sundown. Far as that goes, it got heavy enough by noon, and when we made camp that evening and I took the pack off, I felt my head would shoot up and leave my shoulders from the sudden relief of the load.

I sure had some stiff neck the next morning, and not only the neck but my whole spine, not mentioning my legs and shoulders. I found that out when Bopy called me to breakfast. I'd jerked my head up at his call and I sure answered him back with a squawk. My muscles felt like they'd been jabbed thru with thorns.

Bopy sort of grinned at me and I tried to grin back but I couldn't do that just then. It took me a few minutes to crawl out of the blankets and I was careful not to turn my head in any way. But after

I washed a bit with snow and got something warm under my belt I felt a little better, and I finally returned the grin Bopy had given me when I first woke up.

We left late that morning after I got some of the stiffness out of me, and we traveled slow and easy.

I took on my light pack the next morning. Bopy had made it lighter and I don't think it weighed over ten pounds, and Bopy eased the band on my forehead. I sure flinched under that weight. But, as Bopy thought, that little weight was just the thing to take some of the stiffness out of my neck. And sure enough, it was about gone by noon . . . and stiff again the next morning.

There were many long stiff-neck days for me after that and every day I'd slip under my pack to work out the stiffness I'd got the day before. Finally I got so I could turn my head in the mornings without getting hardly any of the stinging pains, and there wouldn't be any stiffness in my body at all. I was just beginning to get real good when we came to the end of our trail.

[65]

Cowboy in the Making

I was glad when we reached the main camp of Bopy's trap line. But the main camp was a kind of sorry looking sight when we got there. Bopy hadn't been to it for quite a few winters and deep snows had sure laid a heavy hand on it. The roof had caved in, filling the place pretty well up with dirt and raising the dickens with the shelves and everything. The door was down, and there was nothing in the window to keep the breezes and snows from blowing in.

But, as Bopy said, he'd sort of expected that, and that is why he'd come north earlier that year, to fix up the place and be all set again before the furs got good enough to start putting out his traps.

The work of straightening up the camp and making it fit to live in again was sort of interesting to me and I did all I could to help. If I did miss going down to the corrals as I did in the cow camps to the south it wasn't for long. Bopy would watch me and soon give me something to do, something that was most always to my liking.

IX

MY FIRST RIFLE

IT WAS then, when I was about nine years going
on ten, that Bopy found an extra rifle of his. It
was one he'd had in the camp for use in case anything happened to the gun he always carried. The
rifle, being wrapped in canvas, was still in good shape,
and after oiling it, Bopy started to show me how to
handle one of them.

[67]

It was a muzzle loader and about two feet taller than I was. Bopy took a lot of pains showing me how to load it. First a little powder was poured down the barrel from the powder horn. Bopy made sure I understood that there should be very little powder, too much would knock me over and maybe hurt me, he said. After the powder a little piece of paper was tamped in with the long stick that was carried under the barrel. Then about a dozen bird shot were poured in, another wad of paper, and the whole thing tamped again. The only thing to do after that was to pull back the hammer and slip a little copper cap on that little thing that stuck up under it. Bopy told me it was best not to put the cap on till I was ready to shoot.

With a lot of instructions and advice and repeatings of all about a gun and the dangerous end of it, I was finally tried out many times and at last I was told to go ahead and bring home the bacon. "But don't forget what I told you," Bopy said, as a last word.

I remember I was pretty excited when I saw the first thing to shoot at. It was a duck. I missed that

I WAS TOLD TO GO AHEAD AND BRING HOME THE BACON

first one, I couldn't hold that long rifle barrel steady enough and there was no tree near the pond for me to rest it on. The next time or so I had better luck. There was the crotch of a tree for me to use, and I got my duck, but I came near toppling over backwards as I did. I had put in too much powder in reloading. I was more careful from then on.

I had a lot of fun with that rifle, even if I didn't see so much that was worth shooting at. About all I could find was big white rabbits and ducks and things like that. I saw a bear twice, but Bopy had warned me never to shoot big animals, to save them for him because I might spoil the fur and so on. Anyway he had a lot of reasons to give so I wouldn't even try to get the big ones. His main reason, as I found out afterwards, was that so long as I didn't bother the big ones they wouldn't bother me. He knew what might happen if I stirred up a big healthy bear or moose with a load of my little bird shot, and he wanted to make sure I wouldn't rile 'em up that way.

That winter was different than any winter I'd

passed before. We were farther north and the day-light hours were very few. Of course the "Northern Lights" made things pretty bright during the night, but not bright enough so as to make the greased paper window of much use in lighting up the dugout.

The short days and light nights made the winter sort of strange for me. The only place I felt at home was inside. When I did go out it would always have to be on snowshoes. The snow was from four to eight feet deep and I soon lost interest in hoofing it thru timber and more timber. I missed open country. I wanted to see distances and get away from that closed in feeling. What I missed most was going down to some corral and stables. I missed my horses, touching their hides and saddling them up and going some place with bridle reins in one hand and rope in another. So that's why I didn't stay out so much that winter. I'd get homesick. And that's why I stuck pretty well by the dugout, I felt all right there.

I think I drew more horses during the few win-ters I was in that Northern country than I ever did. It seemed like drawing 'em brought 'em nearer to me. If I drew a man on horseback throwing a rope, or doing anything, I'd imagine myself in that picture and doing whatever was put down there. I drew lots of saddles too, and boots and spurs. I'd often draw cattle and most everything that goes with the life of a range rider.

Bopy wasn't with me much that winter, another thing that made the winter different. He'd be gone three days at a time while covering his trap line. When he was gone I'd draw and read and write. There'd be the cooking, too. I was getting to be quite a cook by then and I used to mix up what I thought to be some great baits. The only drawback was that I had to be mighty saving with everything excepting meat; bear and moose. Flour, and things that were heavy to pack, was scarce and not to play with. I was told I could use a certain amount a day and no more. Then there was dried fruit and dried potatoes; good medicine against scurvy. Bopy told me how scurvy killed many Indians and some white folks every winter and how sometimes one little potato could have saved 'em. So I was pretty careful with the dried potatoes and one a day was all I'd cook. Our grub pile was made up of flour, soda, a side of salt pork to season with, dried potatoes and apples, salt and pepper. That was all. Whatever game we killed was our fresh meat and we never were short of that.

I'd feel pretty tickled when I'd manage to cook up something that turned out real good, specially on the evenings of every third day, when Bopy would come in all frozen up with icicles hanging all the way down from his fur cap to his waist. And when he'd rush near the fire to warm up and smell at the pan of food that was on the coals all ready for him and then grin at me and slap me on the shoulder, why I felt that what little I'd done had sure turned out big.

WILL JAMES

X

A BEAR ON THE ROOF

M OST EVERY DAY, while Bopy was gone, and during the daylight hours, I'd strap my snowshoes on my moccasins, take my long rifle and go ahunting, not that I liked to hunt so much, but I wanted to have some reason to be out, and I'd be wanting a change from moose meat. Once in a while

I'd get a big, white snowshoe rabbit. The bears had all hibernated. I hadn't seen a sign of any, *only once.*

It was after a warm spell, a spell that broke that one bear's sleep, and he'd gone out hunting. There was a snow-bank alongside the lean-to where we kept the meat and he'd climbed up on that snowbank on top of the cabin. I heard him sniff and paw up there for a long spell. He was sure heavy because even through that thick roof I could tell just where he planted a paw. Then he must have got a whiff of the meat that was in the lean-to because he kept hanging around there, climbing up and down and clawing. He'd circle around and sniff, and I got to thinking of the window. I hadn't closed the shutter on it and all he'd have to do would be to stick his nose to the paper and it'd fall apart. I knew he'd come in then, so as to get to that meat, and I waited for him.

As I waited I reached for my rifle, not at all realizing that the bird-shot it was loaded with would only make him mad if I did hit him at long distance. Anyway I waited a spell hoping he would stick his nose thru that window. But he didn't. Instead he quit his

FOUND THE BEAR STRETCHED OUT AND FROZEN STIFF

circling and went to tearing at the lean-to as if he sure meant to get that meat. He made plenty of noise and I got to thinking he wasn't doing the house any good, so I ups and slips on my moccasins. I was all dressed but hat, and I opened the door and went out. But I couldn't see the bear and all I could get of his whereabouts was sniffs and grunts. The snow was pretty deep and I couldn't get around very fast, but when I got around the lean-to I met him. He looked like a mountain.

I don't think the barrel of my rifle was over a foot from his nose when I pulled the trigger. Bopy had often told me always to stick the barrel away ahead and be ready for work when I really wanted to use it. It was ahead that night, and I pulled the trigger at just a good time. . . .

When Bopy came back two days later and I told him about the bear, he grinned at me sort of proud-like and said words that made me feel good, on how I'd held down the camp and saved the grub. He said that bears "was awful pests." But if Bopy was surprised and pleased at me getting up in the middle of the night and chasing the bear away, he was more than surprised when he began to track him the next day. He hadn't gone over half a mile from camp when he found the bear stretched out and frozen stiff. That little bird shot at close range had nearly punctured his head through.

Bopy had never thought that I had killed the bear and neither did I. But there he was, and when I came up to answer Bopy's holler and saw that hairy elephant stretched out on the snow I didn't know what to think or say. Bopy said something about a mighty lucky shot and advised me never to try that again with one of those big fellers. He didn't say why right there. But there's one thing Bopy didn't know and that was I'd got to know the old rifle pretty well and I was using twice the amount of bird-shot I'd started out with, and three times the amount of powder. The powder alone would have burned a hole thru him at that close range.

That bear hide would have covered the whole floor of our cabin. It sure was a nice color, too.

XI

GROS AND OTAY

THE CAMP we struck the next winter was quite a camp. It had two rooms and was furnished with things not made out of hewed timber. There were a lot of knickknacks sticking around, too, and pictures of people and some books and things.

I found out that this was Bopy's *one* main camp. It was his home and only about a hundred miles south of where he was born. That camp with all that was in it had a whole lot to do with keeping me contented that winter. There were books and blank paper galore. I could read and draw all I pleased. Then, to make things nicer, I had a couple of pets to keep me company while Bopy was out on his trap line.

My two pets were wolves. The man who brought up our stuff had got 'em out of a den that spring and tried to work 'em in with his dog team. They didn't turn out well as sled dogs and he was going to kill 'em soon as their fur got good. Bopy dickered for 'em and here I was with two big gray fellers following me around. They were well trained and minded me. I didn't take to my pets very much at first, but they sure took to me and wouldn't have hardly anything to do with Bopy. If they did anything I didn't like I'd kick 'em in the ribs, and all they'd do was whine and lie down and beg for me to quit. It strikes me funny when I think of that, because either one of those wolves would just have had to snap at me once and I'd not have been able to touch 'em again. Gray wolves have powerful jaws, and when they stood up on each side of me their withers weren't so far below my shoulders.

I know of one time when Bopy got peeved at something the wolves had done. He hunted 'em up and began to work on 'em. I came about just about when Bopy would soon have been getting the worst of it. He'd got himself a limb off a tree, but it was breaking. Little me ran in and busted up the fight. I kicked each wolf in the jaw and they hunted for a hole as if a ghost was after 'em. Bopy looked at me sort of funny and then he grinned. I had all the handling of the wolves after that.

But kicks weren't all the wolves got from me. The three of us had a lot of fun together. We'd go a-hunting, me with my long rifle and the wolves with their speed and killing power. Sometimes they'd leave me and be gone for hours. They'd be chasing something and come back all gauntled up. In that time I'd killed some meat for 'em and lots of times they'd catch up with me while I was skinning whatever I killed. They'd crowd around me, their long red tongues a hanging, but they never tried to reach for what I had, because they knew what they'd get would be a smack on their long nose. So they'd wait until I got ready and sort of back up against me while waiting. That was their way of hurrying me. A wolf never shows affection—he never licks at a person's face and hands as a dog would and he never wags his tail. The most he does to be friendly is lay his ears back and show a grin and try to look pleasant in that way, like a wolf.

The wolves were a lot of company to me that winter. I called 'em Gros and Otay. They'd lie by me while I drew and read, and I'd never make a move but what they did, too. If I jumped up they'd jump up too, and bustle up and look at the door of the cabin and growl. They'd sure look mean at times and it wouldn't have been so good for anybody to open that door unless he was ready to shoot right quick. Bopy knew that, and he never came in from his trap lines like he used to. He'd whistle a bit first and after he thought I'd got through talking to the wolves he'd ease in, and the tone of his voice as he spoke to me had all to do with his welcome. They never got used to him because he'd be gone too long at a time.

Of course Bopy could have made away with the wolves mighty quick, but seeing how they were so much company for me he figured they were worth

THE WOLVES WERE A LOT OF COMPANY TO ME THAT WINTER

having around. Bopy would laugh when he'd see me and the two wolves all stretched out in front of the fireplace. I'd be drawing while one wolf's head was resting on my leg and the other on my neck.

I didn't care so much for the wolves. Maybe that was why they liked me. I'd kick 'em off and they'd come right back. I'd be drawing horses about then, as usual, and wolf skin wasn't what horse hide meant to me.

Sometimes I'd play the wolves were horses. I'd ride 'em, put hackamores on 'em, and even tried to make pack horses out of 'em. I'd tail one to the other, but they never worked well. They'd slip their packs or else pull out of the hackamore. I'd braided me a four strand rope out of moose hide and I'd throw a loop at them once in a while. They soon got wise to that loop and made themselves hard to catch when they'd see me spread out one.

With that kind of play to hold me I don't think I missed my horses as much that winter as I did the winter before. But I often thought of my little black and sorrel when I threw my moose-hide rope, and

I'd have to draw them once in a while to keep from being too lonely for 'em.

The winter wore on and about February time came along. Moose and caribou were drifting North and one night a pack of wolves went by on their trail. My two wolves were full size by then. They stood up when they heard the drawn out howl of one of their kind, and began to talk back in the same language. They were restless, and figuring on a way out, but I held 'em down that night. It wasn't many nights later, I was sound asleep when I heard something tear. It was the paper on the window, the paper we used instead of glass. My two wolves had jumped up on my bed and gone out.

I listened, and a few seconds later I heard the long holler of a wolf pack. I knew then what had happened. I jumped up, slipped on my long coat and moccasins and went out the way my wolves went. I had my rifle with me and I was going to get my wolves back.

God helps the children and the ignorant, because if the pack had turned I couldn't have written this.

I followed the snarling pack of wolves until I couldn't hear 'em any more. Then, by the night sun, I tracked 'em. I snowshoed and cried and snowshoed and cried some more. I cried because I was peeved to think that Gros and Otay could have left me. I was so peeved at the thought that I'd have been likely to take a shot at them. But, lucky for me, the pack didn't turn—I didn't see my wolves. They had gone with the wild bunch.

It was well along towards sun-up when I dragged my long rifle back into camp. Tears were frozen all along my parka, plum down to my moccasins. Bopy, all eyes and worried, opened the door. He knew what had happened and he spoke soft as he pulled off my cap, unbuttoned my coat, and brought me near the fire.

"Tout est bien, mon enfant" ("all is well, my child"), he said. He slapped me on the shoulder and looked down at me and grinned. "Tu vas avoir tes chevaux bien vite maintenant" ("you're going to have your horses pretty soon, now").

Those words made me perk up, and it wasn't

[89]

long before I began to ask Bopy questions as to how quick that would be. Bopy said, "Bien vite" (pretty soon), and I was put to bed. But I was still hurt. Gros and Otay shouldn't have left me the way they did. I went to sleep on that.

I woke up in a bad humor the next morning. I tracked my wolves some more, but it was no use. By the time I doubled back I think I'd have shot them on sight for running off the way they did . . . I never saw them any more.

True to Bopy's word, we soon drifted south again, and that was good. A squatty musher came to our camp, loaded with furs and bedding and turned his dog team down country. The sight of those dogs, half wolf, made me mad but I soon forgot them in thinking I'd be having my ponies now.

We struck no cow country to speak of that summer, nothing but swampy meadows and high mountains, but I didn't mind so much. It was sure pretty country and I didn't have to walk. My ponies were with me and I'd taken off my moccasins and slipped on my boots. I would be riding again and my heart felt good.

[90]

And there, for this book, the story must end, for it would take too long to tell how I finally got to be on my own and joined first one cow outfit and then another. And as for the story of me and one of my ponies, why that's in another book and I can't tell it again here.

As for my drawing, I never did have any lessons in it and today I draw horses just as Billie did when he was in camp with Bopy—without even looking at 'em.

I'll draw one more for you before I leave off.

WILL JAMES